KWULASULWUT II

More Stories from the Coast Salish

by Ellen White

•

Illustrations by Bill Cohen

Theytus Books, Ltd.

Penticton, British Columbia

THEYTUS BOOKS LTD.
257 Brunswick Street
Penticton, B.C. V2A 5P9

Cover Design, book design and layout: Ande Axelrod

Special Thanks to Regina (Chick) Gabriel, Barbara Helen Hill and Kateri Akiwenzie- Damm.

The publisher acknowledges the support of the Canada Council, Department of Canadian Heritage, the Cultural Services Branch of the Province of British Columbia and the British Columbia Heritage Trust Fund in the publication of this book.

Canadian Cataloguing in Publication Data

White, Ellen, 1922 -
   Kwulasulwut II

   Includes index.
   ISBN 0-919441-54-8

   1. Salish Indians —Folklore—Juvenile literature. 2. Indians of North America—British Columbia—Folklore—Juvenile literature. I. Title.
E99.S2W492 1994   j398.2'09711   C94-910647-X

INTRODUCTION

In 1981, the renowned Salish Elder Ellen White's *Kwulasulwut: Stories from the Coast Salish* was one of the first books to be published by Theytus Books, the first Aboriginal owned and operated publisher to be established in Canada. At that time, the Canadian Book Review Annual wrote "Author White has translated these five children's stories with consummate skill... retaining their simplicity, charm and lyrical quality. The popular children's title is comprised of oral history and transcriptions of five traditional Salish legends."

In 1992, due to demand for a reprint, Theytus published a new edition of *Kwulasulwut* with illustrations by Kwagiulth artist David Neel.

This book, *Kwulasulwut II: More Stories from the Coast Salish*, is a second volume of traditional Salish legends by the Ellen White, with illustrations by the Okanagan artist Bill Cohen. Now Ellen White has interpreted and written down four more Salish legends for this second volume of *Kwulasulwut:* "The Mink and the Raccoon Family," Smuy the Little Deer," "Deer, Raven and the Red Snow," and "Journey to the Moon."

The *Kwulasulwut* series help to fill a gap in that there is relatively little written documentation of Salish legends, yet they are the First Nations whose traditional territory covers most of the Lower Mainland and a large portion of Vancouver Island. In producing this book the publisher has kept in mind that the stories and illustrations are directed primarily at children; but will also have some appeal to adults who will appreciate the cultural and historical aspect.

The author, as a Salish Elder and storyteller, has been trained as a storyteller within the Salish tradition and has had the legends passed on to her.

SMUY, THE LITTLE DEER

Smuy, the little deer, lived in a beautiful valley with his mother and grandfather. There were mountains on both sides and he could see far to the south when he climbed high up into the mountains. He loved to go to the winding river between the mountains. Their little house was set amongst the cedar groves where they could see the river from their house.

Smuy's grandfather was always busy with planting and preparing for the coming season. It was early spring. This was the time for Smuy's training. This time he would learn about water and how to communicate with it. Smuy loved to go to the river and sit on the big branches that stick out over the river banks. This is where he loved to lay on his stomach and lick the water and caress it with his tongue. He would say, "Now look in my eyes little fish and you will swim in them. Come close to me little brothers and sisters because I am going to eat you one of these days and you are going to love it because I love you." He loved to put his little hooves in the water to see the little fish come and circle around them.

Smuy was happy when it was training time because he could talk to all his friends: water, fish, shrimp, and snail. Snail was a lot of fun because Smuy could follow her trail. He would say, "I am going to catch you. I know where you are going." But Snail was very smart. She would circle the trees and say, "Try to find me if you can." Sometimes Smuy couldn't understand what Snail was saying because she spoke in another language. She circled the tree, so he followed. He ran around and around the tree until he was so tired that he lay down to rest. He said to the tree, "Please

2

She circled the tree, so he followed.

help me go to sleep. I am tired." When Smuy fell asleep he sucked the bark of the cedar in his dream and he was refreshed. When he woke up he said, "Hychqa, thank you, tree."

Smuy asked Grandfather, "In your training did you ever believe you could communicate with the trees? Could the tree talk to you?" Grandfather replied, "Do you talk to the trees, grandson?" "Oh yes, Grandfather," said Smuy. "When I fall asleep and dream I say, 'I am so thirsty,' and then the tree gives me water. I can feel water in my mouth. When I wake up I say, 'Hychqa'." Grandfather said, "That is good, my grandson. Never forget to thank the trees for they are there to help us. They will help us but we must ask them for help. We must always honour the trees, the water, and the things that grow and live in the water." Smuy said, "I will always remember to say 'Hychqa,' Grandfather."

Grandfather said, "Now, bring Mother the water that she sent for a long time ago." So Smuy got a little basket of water and carried it home. When he got there he said, "I've got your water, Mother." There was no answer. "Oh, she must be mad at me again," thought Smuy. Mother looked at him and smiled. Then Smuy was happy and did what his mother said, "Eat now, little Smuy. It is going to be a long day and you're going to be gone a long time." When she said that, Smuy knew that Grandfather must have told her it was training time again. He ate very quietly.

When Smuy was done he cleaned his little corner, thanked his mother and left to go to the river to see Grandfather. When he got to the edge of the river Grandfather was there and he said, "Now Smuy, I want you to lay down close to the water's edge and count the water." "Grandfather you can't count the water," Smuy said. "Just look at it and try," replied Grandfather. So Smuy laid on his belly, put his hooves into the water and affixed his eyes

S o Smuy laid on his belly, put his hooves into the water and affixed his eyes very close to the water.

very close to the water. "The water isn't just water anymore. There are a lot of things going on in there," thought Smuy.

Smuy's little friends, the fish knew he was there because they could smell him. The fish said, "Go away, go away, I don't want Grandfather to see you are wasting our time." The fish began to swim by Smuy's hooves and tried to bite at them. There were lots of bubbles. Inside each of the bubbles it was like another world. Smuy was fascinated as he watched the bubbles form.

His grandfather asked Smuy later that day, "Did you look at the water?" "Yes Grandfather I did." "What did you see?" replied Grandfather. "I saw lots of bubbles, Grandfather, they were like long strings of hair. They were floating by and separating. I looked and looked and then snow came along. Beautiful snow. The long strings and snow joined together and formed into long strands and went away. It is like another world in the little bubbles. Sometimes there are faces in there and they're all laughing at me. Why do they laugh at me Grandfather?" Grandfather answered, "They do not laugh at you. They laugh because you are different and they want to get to know you. If they didn't like you they wouldn't be laughing."

Smuy sat quietly and wondered if he could get inside one of those bubbles at least once. But he didn't want to ask Grandfather because he might think Smuy was silly for asking. Just like the time he wanted to be a cricket and Grandfather said, "The way you talk all the time you could be a cricket and the way you jump, you could be a frog." After that Smuy had a weird dream. In his dream he was rolling around by the fire in the middle of the floor. He was awakened when his mother said, "Wake up Smuy, wake up. What is the matter with you?" Smuy replied, "Oh Mother, I had the weirdest dream. I dreamt that I was a cricket. I don't want to dream like that again." His Mother sent him back to bed. "Now you just sleep and don't think of anything," said Mother.

The next morning his Mother woke him early. He got up and followed Grandfather. Smuy was told to go into the water and bathe. "Go forward into the water and come out backward and don't look at me. Keep looking at the water," said Grandfather. The water was so friendly. Smuy loved the water. He wasn't afraid of the water. Smuy went in and then backed up. He did it four times and Grandfather said, "That is enough. Now go and rest in the company of your little Cedar friends and their mother. You might be needing her tomorrow. You must be quiet and rest today. It will be important for you to gather all your energy."

Smuy went into the woods and ran around caressing the little Cedar trees. He told his cedar friends, "I'll be back after I bring Mother some water." He ran to the edge of the stream and filled his little basket with water and than swiftly pranced back to his Mother. He wanted to show off to his little friends how skillfull he was with his basket of water. He balanced it so well that he didn't spill a drop. He looked sideways to see if the Cedars were watching him as he left.

When Smuy arrived home he shouted, "I have your water, Mother." "Hychqa, my son, Hychqa. Now go and eat the tops of the plants in the yard," said Mother. Smuy went out and ate the tops of the plantain plant and flowers of the elders. He had to stretch his little neck to reach the flowers of the tall elder trees, but Smuy made sure he did what Mother said. He knew that Grandfather was on the hill watching his every move. When Smuy was done eating he ran in and out amongst the Cedar trees. Then, continuing his training, he crawled on all fours until he reached the biggest mother tree and announced, "I am here Mother Cedar, please help me.

When Smuy moved away from the tree he thought to himself, " I must be dreaming because the Cedar tree just spoke to me.

Grandfather said I might need you. I don't know what he means, and I'm scared. Make me strong." All of a sudden, Smuy shivered and he didn't know why. He lay close to the tree and sucked the bark. After a few minutes, Smuy took a little bite off the bark and fell asleep.

When he finally awakened he said, "Hychqa, Mother Cedar." Mother Cedar replied, "You're a good little deer. Have a good day." When Smuy moved away from the tree he thought to himself, "I must be dreaming because the Cedar tree just spoke to me. Just like the little fish. I know the fish spoke to me too." As Smuy ran down the hill he said to himself, "I'm not going crazy am I?" When he got to the bottom of the hill, Mother said, "You must be very hungry little one." As Mother gave him some food, Smuy thought, "I am not that hungry. What is wrong with me? I just don't feel like eating." Instead, Smuy took a big drink of his water. There were berries in it and it tasted so good. Smuy could still taste the flowers of the elder trees in his mouth.

That evening Grandfather said to Smuy, "We will not be having our late meal today. Just drink more berry water for now." Smuy drank the water and said, "I am not hungry anyway, Grandfather." Grandfather told Smuy, "That is good grandson, that is good. I will wake you in the morning. Maybe in your sleep, you will find the two peaks you dreamt about." Smuy had told Grandfather about his dream of the two mountain peaks where he believed he would find the Mother Cedar tree. Grandfather said, "You might see her more clearly tonight my grandson." Smuy went to sleep and found himself walking fast, like he was running. No! Just like he was flying. He wasn't touching the ground. He could see the mountains, yet he knew it was dark. He was packing a little sack of dried salmon and Fern roots.

He awakened for a moment to see if he had the dried salmon and roots he had seen in his dream. There beside him were dried salmon and Fern roots that Mother had cooked over an open fire the day before. Smuy wrapped them up and put them under his pillow. As Smuy thought about the food Mother left for him, he slowly drifted back to sleep. In his dream he was on a high ledge behind his house. He could see the two peaks. And there she was - the most beautiful tree. She was the tallest Cedar tree Smuy had ever seen. There were lots of trees surrounding her, but those trees were much smaller than her. Smuy continued to sleep deeply through the night.

In the morning, Smuy was awakened before daybreak. When he heard his little friend, the Wren, chirping in the tree he knew it was going to be daybreak soon. "I am awake so I will go outside now" he said to himself. He crept out of bed so as not to wake Mother and Grandfather. But Mother was very alert, she did hear Smuy and wondered why he was up so early. She was going to tell him to go back to sleep but thought, "Oh I will leave him alone." With her eyes half open she watched him go quietly outside. When Smuy arrived at the opening of the door, Mother could see he was carrying a little bag on his back. She thought to herself, "My son is going away."

Mother did not move but she did send out a prayer for her son. Then she heard another stirring and she knew it was Grandfather. When Grandfather got to the door Mother could see he was also packing something on his back. "Oh, I am so glad Grandfather is going to follow Smuy. Today will be a very quiet day, as well as tonight and maybe tomorrow too," Mother thought. Mother prayed that they would both have a safe journey.

muy went to sleep and found himself walking fast, like he was running. No! Just like he was flying.

"I know Grandfather knows where he is going," thought Mother. Grandfather was not too worried about Smuy either because the night before he had a vision of what Smuy was about to face. Grandfather knew that with the help of daylight or evening light he would be able to see his grandson.

Little Smuy was not tired. Eager to finish his training, he ran until the sun came up and then he found shelter. He took out some of his fish, looked at it and thought, "I am only going to eat a little piece of dried salmon and Fern root. I love eating the black part of the Fern root." He ate and his little mouth got all black. Smuy then laid down and went to sleep. Smuy slept until the afternoon then started running again. When evening came he found a grove of Cedars. He played with the little Cedars first to get to know them. This made them so happy. Smuy wasn't scared anymore. Nor alone. He said, "Hychqa," to his little brothers and sisters, then went to the biggest Cedar and said, "Hychqa, Mother Cedar. I am going to rest here for the night." Mother Cedar smiled and watched Smuy fall asleep under the shining moon.

In his dream, Smuy could see Grandfather running on the upper levels of the hills. He felt that Grandfather must be around. This made him feel very good and he said, "Hello, Grandfather. I can see you. I am so glad you are not too far away. I am going to beat you. I will be far ahead." In the meantime, Grandfather had stopped to rest and when he heard his grandson's voice he smiled. He knew his grandson so well. As Grandfather smiled he thought, "Smuy will grow up to be a fine deer one day. Yes, he will grow up to be a fine deer."

Smuy was up early again the next morning, ready to continue his training. As he started out on his day's journey, he caressed the trees as he

S muy could see Grandfather running
on the upper levels of the hills.

ran by. He played with the smaller trees and hugged them too. He went to the water's edge to look for his little fish and frog friends. They were not there. Smuy ate some dried salmon, licked some water and then started off running again. He thought to himself, "If my training goes on much longer, I will lose track of how many days or nights have gone by."

He wasn't tired but suddenly sensed something familiar. It was the two mountain peaks he had seen in his dream. He thought he could see the trees through the fog and mist. "What is that?" Smuy thought as he looked at the trees in front of him. Smuy started to run fast. He knew he could get to the top before too late in the evening. He was sure to climb carefully as Grandfather had taught him to do. He remembered Grandfather's words, "Watch your footing. Watch where you put your feet. Those are the only feet you have and you don't want to damage them." Throughout his training, Smuy always remembered Grandfather's teachings.

U p ahead there were rocks Smuy had to jump across. Smuy could hear the clicking sound every time his little hooves came in contact with the rocks. "There must have been rock slides here," Smuy thought. Sometimes Smuy would step on a rock and watch it roll away. He was getting higher and higher and knew he was getting closer to the top. Then he came over a little hump and recognized the trees from his dream. It was almost dark again and Smuy had to hurry. As he ran and ran Smuy felt like he was flying. He came to the edge of a forest where the trees were just a little taller than he was. He hugged the closest tree and tears came to his eyes. Joyfully, Smuy said, "I am so glad. I am home. I can rest now." Smuy started playing with the trees. As he moved in further, the trees got taller and rougher as they rubbed against him when he ran by. Sometimes he felt he was about to tumble down a steep hill, but there were trees there to protect him. The trees laughed and played with him too.

Smuy could sense that he was close to Mother Cedar. He said, "I am here Mother Cedar. I am home. I know you can hear me Mother Cedar." To his surprise, he heard Mother Cedar speak, "Rest my son, come closer to me and rest my son." Smuy was so happy he didn't want to question her. He crawled on all fours and snuggled close to Mother Cedar. When he sucked on the bark, he felt nourishment going down into his throat and throughout his body. He stayed there for a long time. It was getting dark again. As the moon began to rise, Mother Cedar said, "Turn your back towards me son, lean against me to get more comfortable."

He found a spot between two roots and leaned up against Mother Cedar. He rested there and began to fall asleep. Just when Smuy started to drift off to sleep he suddenly felt his spine move. He could feel energy moving throughout his whole body. Smuy even felt it tingling down into his hooves. There was so much energy moving around inside him he could hear his spine creaking. He was scared for a second but then remembered Grandfather had told him not to be afraid if anything like this happened.

As he began to relax he felt himself rising upward. He was moving up the tree, gilding up and up. He felt he was doing the right thing . Smuy felt good and warm as he moved slowly upward. He kept moving up and up. He was afraid he would get stuck and thought, "If I get stuck I will not see Grandfather and Mother again." He relaxed and moved further upward. He was afraid to open his eyes but when he did he could see light. When Smuy turned his head he could see the sun going down further and further

He was moving up the tree, gliding up and up.

in the distance. Then he saw something that looked like fog. But it wasn't mist or fog - it could have been a cloud. The clouds came sailing along like they were smiling at him and caressing him at the same time. "This is what I saw!" he said to himself. As the clouds passed, Smuy felt good. He felt as though the clouds had trickled water inside him as they went by. He could see the ocean far, far away.

"Mother is somewhere along those mountains," Smuy thought. He was now on the highest mountain. He was frightened that he would fall and hit bottom and be gone. "Don't be afraid grandson, you are with me, you are alright," whispered Mother Cedar. Smuy became very calm. When he became frightened again he hollered, "Grandfather where are you?" Smuy heard a voice far away in the hills, "Be quiet my grandson. Be calm. You'll be alright. I'm not very far away." Smuy cried, "Grandfather, get me out of here." Grandfather's last words to Smuy were, "No my grandson. Tomorrow we will have a chance to get you out but not tonight. You will learn. Make use of where you are." Smuy stayed where he was but was still afraid.

He was looking up. It was starting to snow. He could feel snow on his little nose. He thought, "I am going to brush the snow away with my little hoof." As he looked down he noticed he didn't have any hooves and screamed, "Where are my hooves? Somebody took my hooves away!" Mother Cedar said, "You are alright my son." Then Smuy relaxed again. When he brought his hooves up he knew they were a branch. He knew he could move his little hooves which were now branches and it would be alright. He slept on and off until he got very thirsty. He whispered, "Mother Cedar, I am thirsty." "Alright my son." That was all Mother Cedar said.

Smuy felt water pour through him. He dozed off again and then he wanted to pee-pee. He said, "Mother Cedar, what am I supposed to do?"

That's alright my son." He felt he was being relieved and everything was alright. Then Smuy wanted to go poo-poo in the middle of the night and thought, "No I can't do that! What am I going to do?" Mother Cedar said to him, "We are one. Remember we are the trees, you are one with us. While you are here everything is alright." When Mother Cedar was through speaking Smuy felt relieved. He felt so good he fell back to sleep. Smuy enjoyed the wind. It was just like he was laying back in the river, rolling in and out. He could feel the rain and the mist. It felt so good and warm on his face. Smuy thought, "It must be cold." Yet Smuy felt good. "I am going to enjoy you and love you Mother Cedar and all the beauty that surrounds me while I am here," spoke Smuy.

He awakened the next morning and saw light. There was a light coming from the water far away. Smuy realized it was the sun. The sun was coming out of the water. When the light started to come out Smuy saw another light coming from behind him. It was another sun coming from the other mountain peak. As both suns moved over the horizon Smuy could see their rays start to roll like a big tunnel towards him. He watched in amazement as the two rays of sun met him. He prepared himself as they came closer. He heard Mother Cedar somewhere in his mind saying, "Be strong my son, be strong."

He watched the two rays of sun meet and when they met there was an explosion of bright light that hit him and the top of the tree. He was worried Mother Cedar would be injured. She said, "I am alright." The instant he heard this he started to slide ever so slowly - down, down, down. His little hooves tried to stop him as he caressed the tree. But he knew he must go. He would not be sad because he had gotten to visit Mother Cedar. He wasn't too far from the bottom. He could see the tops of the small trees

As both suns moved over the horizon Smuy could see their rays start to roll like a big tunnel towards him. He watched in amazement as the two rays of sun met him.

near the bottom. Smuy saw his body too. "What am I doing down there? Why am I down there? Why is that so?" thought Smuy. He said to himself, "It must have been my soul that was inside Mother Cedar." He knew this was true as his little hooves touched his little head and went inside his body. He didn't struggle and he fit back into his body perfectly.

He got up, shook himself, and thanked Mother Cedar. Smuy touched Mother Cedar with his head and ran off happily. He touched the other trees, making noises as he went. They swished and touched his back. Pretty soon he was in the middle of the softest trees - the little ones. He rolled by them and caressed them as he laughed with them. He nibbled on the ends of their limbs as he talked with them. Then he rolled down the hill. There was a little bit of snow on the ground and he rolled into the snow happily.

Grandfather sat up in the hills and watched and prayed. Grandfather thanked Mother Cedar and the others for taking care of Smuy. He thanked the two peaks for helping bring the vision to his grandson. He was grateful that his power had matched the sun's strength so his grandson could be released from the tree. "I'll just sit here and watch and enjoy him being a little boy for now," whispered Grandfather. Smiling, Grandfather said, "Yes, play my grandson, play like a little boy. For tomorrow you will be a man."

Grandfather went to meet his grandson and said, "Come, my grandson. We shall eat in the next rise of hills and bathe in the streams and then prepare to go home to your mother." They collected little salmon in the streams to bring home to Mother. Smuy was very happy to go home. "Hychqa, Grandfather, Hychqa", said Smuy.

C ome, my grandson. We shall eat in the next rise of hills and bathe in the streams and then prepare to go home to your mother.

JOURNEY TO THE MOON

In a small village lived a young man from the Crow Family, a royal family. Because he was from a royal family he was guarded, watched, and well trained. He was going to marry a beautiful young woman from the next village. She was also was from the Crow Family. Her village was one day away or, as the elders would say, "one day's run" away. The young woman was highly trained in all spiritual teachings.

The young woman always talked about going to the moon. She said she heard voices from the moon asking her to come and stay with them. If she did decide to go, she was told she would become their queen. She bragged to her sisters and cousins that one day she would go to the moon and become a queen. Of course nobody believed her. They thought she was just bragging.

The young man, her fiance, told his brothers and cousins about her belief that she would one day go to the moon. His cousins always teased him by saying that he was going to have to go to the moon to collect his bride.

In the young woman's village, the grandfathers and grandmothers said it was time for the young women to spend several nights in the forest as part of her training. The old ladies assisted the young women and stayed close to them in the forest. They taught the young women about the forest. Stories were shared throughout the day, while the evenings were spent cleansing.

The young woman always talked about going to the moon. She said she heard voices from the moon asking her to come and stay with them.

After a long day of training, the young women laid upon the open field of grass and looked up at the stars and moon. Before they went to sleep, the young woman told the others that the man in the moon was talking to her. "He is talking to me now. I know his voice. Can't you hear him?" said the young woman cheerfully. The young woman's cousins laughed and said, "Oh yes, we can hear him." The young woman replied, "Oh good, oh good. I knew you would hear him. He wants me to go there and become his queen. I can't believe he wants me to go there. I can't wait." This went on for two nights.

On the second night one of the old ladies said, "Let's try to sleep tonight instead of laughing and chattering about going to the moon." The young women giggled and chuckled as they lay beneath the star filled sky and the moon. One of the old ladies heard them and softly spoke, "Ssshh, lay there – count the stars and look at the moon, this will help you to sleep." A few minutes passed and another old lady whispered the story of when people journeyed to the moon long ago . The young woman whispered to her sisters and cousins, "Did you hear that? They did journey to the moon and I'm going to journey there too." They didn't want to listen to her anymore and with loud yawns and sighs of relief, they laid their heads on their little mats. Their sleepy eyes continued to look up at the stars and the moon. They tried to count how many mountains were on the moon and soon fell asleep.

Shortly after, one of the sisters screamed, "Wake up! Wake up! What is happening to our sister?" The young woman was facing up with her eyes closed. There was steam coming from her body. It thickened like fog as it hovered over her. Slowly, the fog formed an image in the shape of her body. The young women assured themselves not to move and that everything would be alright. But all of a sudden, the image of the young woman turned and started heading upwards. They ran and told their grandmothers.

Before the grandmothers could even speak, their eyes quickly turned to watch the image of their granddaughter going up into the sky. The young woman's image didn't go straight to the moon, instead it seemed to go in the direction of the young man's village. As this image of her disappeared, the old ladies ran to her body. They agreed not to touch her but to cover her instead. "She'll be alright as long as we don't touch her. We must tell grandfather," said one of the old ladies. A runner amongst the young women was sent to inform grandfather.

In the meantime, in the village of the young man, voices could be heard. The young men too were counting the stars and looking for mountains on the moon. The young man softly spoke, "My fiance said there are big lakes and rivers inside the moon. Families who live there only come out once a day." The brothers and cousins smiled. They didn't believe that to be true. Just at that moment, one of the brothers said, "Look! Look what's coming." They all sat up and watched a fog-like image come towards them. It hovered above them.

One of the cousins said, "It looks like the shape of your fiance." It hovered closer to the young man, circled and then went directly up towards the moon. "What are you going to do?" his brother said. The young man said, "I must go. I must go to her parents and grandparents." The boys said, "You cannot go. You would not be allowed to go unless you go with an adult." The young man said, "Well, come with me then. All of you. That way, we'll all be together." They ran the rest of night until they reached the young woman's village.

B ut all of a sudden, the image of the young woman turned and started heading upwards.

At daybreak the young men came to a clearing just above the young woman's village. There they found one of her male cousins. He was sitting on the edge of the clearing crying. The young man asked, "What's wrong?" "I'm not allowed to say," he replied. "Alright then, " said the young man, "I must go and see your grandparents."

It was early morning when the young man ran into the village. Outside the house of the grandparents, the family was together crying and holding hands. The young woman's grandfather said to him, "You have come. We must tell you that your fiance is gone. She got her wish. She has gone to the moon." The young man said, "All of her... or just...?" The grandmother said, "No, her body is here and well taken care of. But her soul is gone." The other elders sitting there asked, "How did you know to come here?" With a shaking voice, the young man said, "She visited us. She hovered just above us and we saw it was her. Then she went straight up towards the moon." Grandfather spoke, "You're our only hope of getting her back. You are trained. You are trained not to lose your breath when you hit the dead world. Because she is promised to you, you are the only one who'll be allowed to enter the outer world of the moon. You must go to her now and bring her back."

The grandparents walked quickly into the forest and came out at the clearing where the young woman's body was. The young women sat huddled together on one side of their sister's body and the young men sat on the opposite side. The young man wanted to go to her quickly; but first, grandmother needed to put some red ochre onto his chest. She gave him a mat. He took the mat and spread it alongside the young woman's body. He laid down beside her and looked up at the stars and moon. He started counting the stars and tried to find the mountains in the moon. He did this over and over. As he prayed his arms felt very heavy but just as quickly he felt very light, as if he were flying.

The young men and women noticed the fog starting to form a cloud around the young man. The cloud covered his body, turned him and carried his body directly up into the sky. As the young man travelled up into the sky, the old people started to cry. The young man knew he was getting very heavy as he neared the dead world. He had heard so much about it. The young man breathed in remembering that he must care for his soul. He felt light as a feather drifting upward, as he continued to look at the moon.

The young man finally arrived at the moon. He didn't want to go to the bright side of the moon instead he wanted to land on the dark side. As he landed, he heard someone speak, "You are here my grandson?" He was surprised to find a grandmother there. This old lady was spinning wool-like stuff on her bare knee. The young man's eyes adjusted to the semi-darkness and then looked closer at the old lady. The young man silently thought, "Ohhhhh, there are many...many knees." The young man quickly realized that this was a Spider Lady. All her arms were working in harmony. She grabbed the wool-like stuff and spun it into fine threads which filled a basket on her right side.

The young man stood behind her for a while and watched her work. She was not surprised. She said, "I knew you were coming. I've been waiting for you. To ease your worried mind, I will tell you that the young woman you've come for is in there." One of her arms pointed towards the

H e felt light as a feather drifting upward,
as he continued to look at the moon.

mountain. "If you think she's the queen, you're wrong. She's not a queen in there." He asked, "Is she alright?" Spider Lady gave a nod of uncertainty. "Can I go in there?" eagerly asked the young man. She nodded, "Yes, but for now go rest on that rock." He went to sit down on the rock and looked around in amazement. There was dust everywhere. It was a fine, light foamy dust-like fog. Spider Lady said, "If you are hungry, my grandson, eat some of it. It will give you energy." He didn't want to try it, but he did. It tasted very good. The light, foam-like dust felt like liquid but it wasn't liquid and it felt solid but it wasn't solid.

Spider Lady, busily working said to him, "You will have to hide. Soon they will come from inside and if they see you here, they will kill you." She turned to look at him and said, "You are too round. You will not fit into the cracks of these rocks." She motioned with one of her arms towards a crack in which he would have to hide. He looked at her and said, "I can't go in there." Spider Lady replied, "You must bring forward the thought of what you are thinking." He thought about this for awhile. The young man silently questioned, "The thought of what you are thinking?" Looking down beside herself, the Spider Lady said, "He will show you." Sitting beside her was a mouse, almost the size of a rat. The mouse whispered, "Come my little brother, I will show you." The mouse hopped along and the young man followed. He heard the Spider Lady say, "I will call for you when it is time for you to come out."

The young man followed the mouse and when he got to the crack he thought to himself, "What did Spider Lady say?...Bring forward the thought you are thinking." The young man said out loud, "I want to be very thin." All of a sudden he was as light as and as flat as a clam shell. Really flat. He felt he could blow away. His little mouse friend grabbed the corner of the

30

One of her arms pointed towards the mountain.

flat disk he had become and helped push him through the crack in the wall of the mountain. Suddenly, the young man was in the crack. He said, "I fit and I feel good. I'm not cold and I feel safe." The young man felt his little mouse friend petting him and heard him say, "Go to sleep." The little mouse filled the cracks with dust so nobody could see the young man. The young man was encased in the crack of the mountain.

While the young man was in the crack, he thought about a lot of things..."The mountain might shake and rumble and I might be squished inside here...I'm already very thin, but then I would become nothing. If this mountain was to shake and crumble...I would be like dust on the surface of this moon." He said to himself, "I remember what the moon looked like as I was descending and coming closer and closer to it. I saw great big puckered lips looking at me and I wondered which puckered lip I was going to land in. I remember landing in one big hole. It was like the puckered lip I saw when I was arriving on the moon. I remember landing on the soft dust-like surface. That was when I heard the Spider Lady speak to me."

The young man thought..."How am I going to get my fiance home?" He thought of his own parents. He didn't get to say goodbye to them or his grandparents. "What are they thinking of me now? But what could I do? The young woman's family said that I was their only chance of bringing their granddaughter safely back home. I knew I had to do this regardless of whether or not I lived." Then he thought..."My body isn't so far away. I know it's my soul that brought me here." His soul lightened as his thoughts drifted in and out of his mind, slowly laying him down to rest.

The young man didn't know how long he slept. He was awakened by someone tickling his toes. His little mouse friend said, "Wake up. Wake up. The doors are going to open. Spider Lady said you must wake up

S uddenly, the young man was in the crack.

now." The young man shook the sleep from his head and felt the mountains shake. He was too scared to worry. "Don't come out yet. We must wait until Spider Lady says it is alright," whispered the little mouse. A few minutes later, Spider Lady motioned for them to come out. The young man jumped out. As soon as he was out of the crack in the mountain, he returned to his normal shape again.

The young man started to run. His little mouse friend followed behind swinging his tail close to the ground to cover their tracks. They ran to where Spider Lady was sitting. Spider Lady acted like she didn't see them. She lifted the basket of foam and told them to jump in. They jumped into the basket and were covered in foam. The young man peeked out. He looked at the mountain as its big doors started to open. As the doors opened, little humans started running out. They were carrying little baskets of the same light dust-like foam Spider Lady was weaving. As they were running and scooping the foam off the surface of the moon, they were eating some of it too.

Spider Lady didn't look at them. She continued to spin the wool into fine threads. The little mouse jumped up and said, "Follow me. I will look after you. We must look after one another." As they ran the little mouse friend continued to sweep his tail close to the ground to cover their tracks. They hid behind a huge rock by an opening in the mountain. The young man said, "I'm going to go through the opening." The little mouse said, "Oh no. You can't go in yet. There are many guards behind that opening." The young man stopped and thought for a moment. "Okay, let's go around to that big rock to the left." So they quickly scurried to the big rock and to their amazement they saw a big hole. They crawled into the hole and saw the side of the mountain. They saw many rivers and trees. In the distance, the young man saw smoke coming from a firepit. There were no dust particles there. It looked like Mother Earth; a little different, but it felt and looked familiar.

The young man and his little mouse friend walked to a river across from the village where the young man had seen smoke. There the little mouse said, "This is as far as I can take you. I will wait here for you. You must cross the river by yourself." On the shore there was an old and tattered little canoe. The young man hopped into the little canoe and started to paddle across the water. On the other side, the little canoe got stuck amongst some rocks. The young man was wondering what to do about the little canoe. Just then the little canoe said to him, "It will be alright. I will wait here for you."

When the young man arrived at the edge of the village he noticed that some of the ladies were cooking. They looked almost human; but they were talking in a strange language. When the young man concentrated hard enough, he was able to understand what they were saying. They said, "Oh yes, you must bring a bowl of this to our leader. He will love it. She will love it too." And they laughed and laughed, and they said, "She claims she is the leader's beloved and she is not. Why would he tie her up if she was the beloved one?" They continued to laugh. The young man snuck up alongside the edge of a nearby wall, as he didn't want the ladies to see him. He heard screaming, "I don't want any of you near me. You are all ugly and I am so beautiful . When I am married to the master, I will punish you all."

The young man thought to himself, "That must be her. I recognize her voice." He went further along the edge and looked over the other side of the wall. There she was, all tied up. He quickly went to her side and said, "Stay quiet and I will release you. If I am too slow untying you, we'll be in

trouble and I'll have to hide in the woods until they leave us alone again."
He heard the voice of his little mouse friend, "There won't be a next time.
You must release her now and both come quickly."

The young woman said, "I will never go with you. Do you know I am
the most beautiful, most wanted person here? They love me. Why would I
want to go with you?" Speaking softly, the young man said, "So why are
you tied up if you are what you say you are?" "They are so afraid I will
leave them, they protect me this way," replied the young woman.

The young man didn't believe her. He said, "I am going to release you
and you are going to come with me or we will both be dead." Raising her
voice, the young woman said, "They won't kill me. I am the most loved
person here." He grabbed her, threw her over his shoulders and started to
run. The ladies cooking nearby saw this and they laughed and clapped their
hands. The young man heard them say, "There! Somebody wants you.
Somebody does like you. We don't have to feed you and your screaming
mouth anymore."

The young man ran until he got to a little canoe in the water. The little
canoe slid from the rocks and the young man jumped In. He didn't seem
to use the paddles this time. The young woman was still kicking and
screaming. Once on the other side of the water, the young man thanked the
little canoe. In slow motion the canoe glued itself back onto the rocks. The
little mouse friend was there to greet them. They started to run. The young
man began to tire and his little mouse friend grabbed the young woman,
put his hand over her mouth and ran with her. As they ran, she mumbled,
"You stink. I don't want to be packed by you. Let me down."

As they approached the mountain where the hole was, they crawled

The ladies cooking nearby saw this and they laughed and clapped their hands.

37

along praying the young woman wouldn't make any noise. They found the hole in the mountain and crawled through to the other side. "Phew, we made it," sighed the little mouse, as they continued running.

When they arrived closer to Spider Lady, she motioned towards the cracks in the mountain. "You must go in there and look at your home!" As he looked, the young man saw a great big shiny ball coming towards them. It was the Earth. Spider Lady said, "It is too far away yet. Besides, the people from inside the mountain are still out. You must go back into the cracks of the mountain until all of the people are back inside. By then your home world will be closer and I'll be able to help you down." The young man grabbed his fiance. When he thought of becoming thin, instantly, they both became thin. The young man pulled the young woman towards him and they went into the crack of the mountain. As the young woman fell asleep, the young man prayed she wouldn't wake up and start screaming.

Later, the young man heard his little mouse friend approaching and saying, "Spider Lady wants to see you now." The young man slid from the crack, pulling his fiance with him. He thought of them returning to their normal forms and "poof" they were heavy again. They ran and the little mouse covered their tracks. The young man looked back at the crack of the face on the mountain. He thought, "How could I have gotten in there?" He thanked the crack of the mountain and continued to run.

As the young man neared Spider Lady he heard her say, "Your home is beneath us now. See it?" The young man said, "Yes, I see it." The young man thought, "I don't know what I'll do with her." Just then, Spider Lady took a chunk of the thread she had woven and wrapped it around the young woman's feet. Spider Lady said, "I'm going to tie her on the end of this rope and let you down together. You're going to fall but you'll be

S pider Lady said, "I'm going to tie her on the end of this rope and let you down together.

comfortable as you fall because you'll still be tied to me." As they were let down it felt very comfortable. Spider Lady said, "If I pull twice that means everything is fine and I will release you shortly thereafter. If I pull once, we have been found out. The first place they'll look for the young woman is here with me. I will then have to drop the rope. Try to wrap yourself with the rope as you fall. That way, when you land, you'll be all wrapped up. You'll be alright. You'll be wrapped like a cocoon and you'll be able to breathe again once you enter the world of the living."

The young man was so afraid as they started going down. The young woman started to kick. They went down further and further. The young woman screamed and pulled to try free her hands. The young man told her, "Don't scream. I'm going to try to get you home. Your parents and grandparents want you to come home." She said, "Your grandparents are so ugly. Your parents are so stinky. Your mother is so ugly." He didn't say anything because she had already loosened the ropes. The young woman hollered, "I am going to go back. I'm going back." The young man responded, "Spider Lady said you can't go back because they don't want you back there." The young woman then replied, "She's not my grandmother. She's too ugly to be my grandmother and I don't care what she says."

Just then the young woman let go of the ropes and drifted away. As she floated away the young man tried to catch her. He swayed as far as he could and prayed but still he couldn't reach her. The last he saw of her was her little mouth chattering and her legs still kicking. She floated over the horizon.

All of a sudden the young man felt the rope jerk once and he knew they had been found out. He started turning as he was instructed. He turned to the right a few times and kept rolling his body into the rope. He was quickly beginning to form his cocoon. He wasn't completely wrapped when all of a

S*he floated over the horizon.*

sudden there was a big thud. He hit air. It took a while before he could breathe. He kept rolling his body into the rope. Still drifting, the young man felt another thud and knew he was home.

The young man was lying beside the young woman's body. Time passed and the grandfather said, "Are you in there grandson?" The young man said, "Yes I am. I am here grandfather." The young man was happy. It was his own grandfather. "Stay really still, grandson. We are going to open one end of what you are wrapped in, so we do not ruin it, and we will pull you out," said his grandfather. The young man could hear the old ladies talking to him, "Breathe very lightly." He knew then that he was home. The grandmothers and grandfathers lifted him up. They laid him right down in the place where his grandmother had painted him with red ochre. The young man disappeared with a swishing sound and instantly he was inside his own body. He sat up and saw the cocoon beside him. His grandfather told him not to look to the right where the young woman lay. He then helped pull his grandson away.

When they returned to the young woman's village, the young man saw his fiance covered and ready for burial. The family consoled him and said, "You have tried. You worked very hard for us. We will save the material you brought home. You will know what to do with it when the time is right. You might use it for your home; but not now. Now you will go up to the mountain and stay with your cousins." The family assured the young man, "She will be alright. We will lay her to rest. You must forget her now."

Up in the mountains, his cousins asked what happened and he told them his story. The young man told them what it was like on the moon. He quietly spoke, "all of the mountains you see on the moon from here on earth are really mountains with puckered lips." The cousins just smiled and continued to stare up into the sky. They couldn't imagine what it was really like on the moon but they respected their cousin and knew it was time for his healing. The young man watched his cousins sleep and knew he loved them very much. He looked up and thanked the stars, the moon and his friends, Spider Lady, his little mouse and the mountain for the sacred time he spent amongst them. The young man was thankful for being home with his family.

THE MINK FAMILY AND
THE RACCOON FAMILY

This story takes place on a beautiful long bay where the water's edge meets the low tide. On one side of the bay lived a family of Mink and on the other side lived a family of Raccoons.

The Mink were a very clean family. They were well trained and well mannered. The parents taught their children about plants, shrubs, trees and how to respect their surroundings. The Mink parents picked a beautiful spot among the rocks for their home. "This cave is a perfect home for us," said father Mink. "It has four holes in the rocks just the right size to store our goods." Their goods were stored to be eaten later. Outside their home was kept clean. There was no garbage anywhere. They put the garbage they collected from the water back into the water where it came from.

One morning father Mink was up very early. As he looked across the bay he thought to himself, "How pitiful it is the way the Raccoon family lives. I feel so sorry for the three children they have. They are brought up with no training and look at the garbage they live in. The children never get up in the morning with their parents. They don't get out of bed and their parents are tired of trying to wake them up." Father Mink thought, "I must do something about this. Maybe I can help."

Grandfather Sun was just coming up over the horizon and the Mink family was already up. Father Mink went up to their home and said, "My dear wife, it is time to get the children up." "Yes, my dear husband," she said. "Get up now children. Your father said it is time to go, we must find

44

A s he looked across the bay he thought to himself,
"How pitiful it is the way the Raccoon family lives."

45

food for the day. But first, you must eat your little goodies that you have saved. There are tasty legs of crabs and little fish heads and tails that have been washed." The Mink children enjoyed every tasty little morsel.

When they finished eating father Mink looked at them and he said, "You know what to do?" "Yes father, we know what to do." They went down to the beach and washed their hands with salt water. The children had to thank the salt water. The children spoke, "Hychqa (thank you) for letting me wash my hands. Here's an offering of goods so you may have a taste too." When they finished washing, they joined their parents. After a quick inspection of the children's hands, mother Mink handed a basket to each of the children. Father Mink said, "Say good morning to the plants my children." "Good morning plantain. How many frogs did you put to bed in your beautiful leaves last night?" chattered the children. The children knew that Plantain was used for frog beds. Their nice large leaves made a perfect shelter for the frogs. When it rained, the rain rolled off leaving the little frogs dry.

Mother Mink said, "Take a leaf and put it on the bottom of your baskets to keep as medicine. If you get a stomach ache, reach into your goodie basket, tear off a piece of the plantain leaf and chew on it. This will help relieve your stomach ache. It's also good to chew if you have a toothache." Mother Mink also noticed some yarrow. It smelled good. Eaten with other foods it made good medicine for sore throats. Mother Mink told the children to take a little stem to put into their baskets. "Say Hychqa to Mrs. Yarrow!" mother Mink said. "Hello Mrs. Yarrow," said the children sheepishly. Mother Mink assured the children that sore throats get scared and that they run and hide from Mrs. Yarrow. The children's eyes beamed as they finished placing a stem of yarrow into their baskets.

Father Mink told the children to walk ahead. He figured it was good for the children to take the lead. He said to his eldest son, "You be the leader today. Take us to where the tasty little fish and nicest little clams and crabs are." As they followed the leader they started finding mussels - mussels are cousins to clams. Mussels are a different colour than clams and are very sweet. They don't last very long, so they have to be eaten right away. It's best to dig the little clams when the tide goes out. After the Mink family washed the sand from the little clams, they ate the biggest part and saved the nose to eat later. "Oh these clams are so sweet. We just love these clams," said the Minks with their mouths full.

The Minks continued to look for the little fish. Father Mink said, "Remember what you have to do! Walk quietly and slowly down the beach. If you step on the barnacles, especially the round barnacles, it would make a loud noise and scare away the fish. "It's not good to scare the fish. If you scare them, they will tense and their meat will sour in your stomach. You wouldn't be able to sleep." They walked ever so slowly towards the water's edge and sat with their little toes in the water.   The mink chanted, "Come on little fish. Can you hear my stomach? It wants to eat you. Come on. Come close to my hands." The Minks saw fish swim closer and closer and pretty soon they started nibbling on the Minks' toes. Softly saying, "Hychqa, Hychqa," the Minks' hands went slowly into the water. The fish thought the fur covered hands were something delicious to eat. Two or more little fish swam towards the Minks' little hands, and with a quick, quiet swish, the little Minks clasped their hands shut. Slowly lifting their hands up from the water, the Minks peeked into their hands to see how many fish they had caught. Fishing for the little Minks was not complete until the last Mink was able to catch some.

The Minks saw fish swim closer and closer and pretty soon they started nibbling on the Minks' toes.

48

In the meantime, Father Mink watched and smiled at his family while they practiced fishing. Mother Mink went to her own little spot to fish. She knew she had to get more fish than she needed. She shared with her husband, as he was too busy training the children. When the children got the fish they needed for that day, they went to a pond where there were no fish and clams. They sat comfortably in the pond and washed the few fish they had caught. After washing the fish, the little Minks ate the fish, except for the fish heads. They saved them to eat later. Once the little Minks finished eating they washed their soiled hands and mouths clean. They did this so the flies would not swarm them.

From time to time, father Mink told the little children how the water protected all the good things to eat. He once said, "The water helps move the food from one area to the next, so the clams and little fish have food to eat. The barnacles don't have legs or fins to paddle themselves around, so they stay in one area and wait for food. The water brings them food. As for the mussels, they cling to rocks and are fed food the water brings. The ocean brings a fresh supply of food."

The children thanked the fish, "Hychqa. My stomach thanks you. My stomach feels so happy and full." The old lady fish said, "I am so glad that my grandchildren fish have been used. We are very happy that you selected us to eat. We are honoured to share with you."

Father Mink told the children, "The mussel and clam shells must be left where they've been dug up. The shells must stay here. The fish bones must be put back into the water too. This is where they live." The Mink children pushed the shells down into the sand so they wouldn't float away. As the children placed the shells into the sand, they said, "These shells are so beautiful mother, can we take them home?" Mother Mink said, "If there is

49

T he old lady fish said, "...We are honoured to share with you."

something you can use them for and if you really need them, then it would be alright." The children looked at one another and thought about how they could use the shells. The children thought they could use them to sail as boats in the pond beside their house. They asked mother Mink if they could take a shell each. "Alright, but you can only take one shell each," replied mother Mink. "Hychqa, mother. Hychqa. We will look after them!" screamed the children. The children put the shells upside down in the water and sailed them. They competed with one another by seeing which shell would win.

Mother Mink was busy picking camus. The camus were quite large and big like onions. She said, "We only need to eat two of these for now and I will dry the rest for later." She took some Fern roots and started to dry them too. Mother Mink replied, "These roots will be dried for winter use. It's important to gather foods now, and to get them ready for the winter." When the Mink family finished preparing the roots, they went into the woods and relaxed amongst the trees. Snuggled up amongst a cool dry stump, father Mink said with a yawn, "We will bring the goods home after we've rested for awhile."

On the other side of the bay, father Raccoon was tired of hollering at his boys. He told his wife, "Go wake them. I am not going to bother with them. You wake them up." Grandfather Sun was not too high in the sky yet, but it was getting late in the day for children to still be sleeping. Mother Raccoon went into the little house. She didn't want to bother with the children either. She too was tired of trying to get them up but she hollered out, "You heard your father. Your father is very tired of trying to wake you up. You must get up and help us gather food for the day." "Oh go away," one of the children said. "We just want to sleep. Don't bother us. We don't have to eat." Mother Raccoon was tired of the children's bickering. She picked up her basket and followed her husband. Father Raccoon already went ahead on the trail to look for a good place to find clams and mussels.

When father Raccoon found a clam or mussel, he grabbed it and smashed it on the rocks. He sucked the juice from the shell and threw it down without putting it back into the sand where they lived. The tide was quite low and father Raccoon put his long fingers into the rocks where he could catch little crabs. He shoved the crab into his mouth and started chewing. Father Raccoon slobbered all over his chin and then spit the rest of the crab on the rocks.

Father Raccoon travelled along to the point of the bay. He stood there and looked over to the other side of the bay and saw the Mink family going up into the trees. He thought to himself, "They're going up into the trees and the sun isn't even high yet. They're so lazy, they don't even want to stay and gather their food." Father Raccoon didn't know that the Minks had been up for a long time. He went to the water and caught some little fish and threw them up onto the rocks. Father Raccoon found some mussels, clams and crabs too. He knew he had to hang on tight to the crabs because they were quick and could run away from him. He sat there and started eating his shells and crabs. From time to time he would look up to see whether mother Raccoon was coming behind him.

Mother Raccoon caught some crabs too. She liked the delicate shells

O h go away," one of the children said. "We just want to sleep. Don't bother us. We don't have to eat."

53

and crabs. She sat quietly, cleaning and eating the shells and crabs. She heard father Raccoon eating and thought to herself, "Why does he make all that noise when he eats?   He's going to scare all the other food around him away. No wonder he's always angry. Maybe he's got a sour stomach and maybe the bones from the fish get stuck in his teeth too." Just then, father Raccoon looked over at his wife and grumbled to himself, "There she sits, she thinks she is so clean and beautiful and that all those little fish will come swimming to her. The way she is thanking them doesn't mean much because one can't thank anything that is already dead. She's not so clean. I can smell her from here." Mother Raccoon saved some of her goods for herself and the children. She thought to herself, "If they are good then I'll share with them. The children will have to gather water and clean where they slept in order to get something to eat."

Out by the water's edge, father Raccoon shoved all the broken crab, clam and mussel shells into his basket. He thought, "Those children don't know how to clean food, these shells must be broken up so they can get at the food more easily." He looked at his wife and thought.. "She's taking her time and I'm slaving away. She probably wouldn't even rub my sore back. She doesn't know how heavy this basket can get." Mother Raccoon continued to follow father Raccoon. She didn't need to know where father Raccoon was going because she could smell and follow the drippings from his food basket. Mother Raccoon was sure to keep her basket clean, she didn't want any strangers to rob her food.

When father Raccoon arrived at home he thought, "I know the children will still be sleeping in the stinky place they slept in last night. How can they stand sleeping in those stinky beds?" Right outside their house, among the rocks, there was a pile of food from three days before. It smelled so bad that coming around the edge of the point one could smell the stink from that pile. Father Raccoon dumped the fresh broken shells and other food on top of yesterday's garbage and threw his basket amongst the rocks. He looked at mother Raccoon and said, "You tell the children the food is there. I don't even want to bother to speak to them." Mother Raccoon told the children, "Your father brought back some food for you." The children replied, "Where is yours? We want yours too!" She told the children, "I will share mine with you when you do something good for me." The children smirked, went outside and started picking at the pile. "OOoo I got yesterday's food. It tastes horrible. I'm not going to eat this anymore. I'd rather starve," said the children, as they mixed and played with the food. The freshly gathered food got mixed up with the staled food.

Mother Raccoon said, "I'm taking my basket and I'm going into the hills to find some roots to go with the rest of the food." "We want your food," cried the little Raccoons. Mother Raccoon told her children, "When grandfather water comes in, it will be too late to get anymore food for the day." Mother Raccoon heard the children hollering as she went into the woods, "We're hungry, mother!"

The Raccoon children were angry and upset at their parents, at the water, and at the pile of garbage outside their house. The children sat by the water and one of them said, "You know what? The other day when I was on the other side of the bay where the Mink family live, I saw holes in the rocks. I think they sleep there and keep their goods there too. We can go over there and get some if you want. I don't think they even eat their

I'm not going to eat this anymore. I'd rather starve," said the children, as they mixed and played with the food.

food. I noticed that they washed their food then put it into the rocks? Maybe they put their food there for us to eat." They all laughed and ran towards the water. Every day for the next few days, the Raccoon children sneaked away to the other side of the bay until they found out where the Minks hid their food.

Early the next morning father Mink was up early as usual. Every day he went down to the beach and washed his hands and face. He always thanked the water for the new day and prayed to the water to look after his wife, children and himself. As he walked along he saw some of the goods they had gathered, scattered out upon the beach. He was very upset about this, as he gathered and placed what was left back into the water.

Father and mother Mink decided it was time to sit down and have a talk with their children. When the children awakened mother Mink said, "Your father and I want to talk to you." The children got up, fixed and cleaned their sleep area, and quickly went to wash up. When they arrived back at their house, mother Mink asked them to sit down. Father Mink started off by saying, "We don't want you taking too much food if you are not going to eat it all. We saw some food scattered on the beach this morning."

The children looked at one another and one of them said, "But father, we thought you and mother got hungry during the night and borrowed some of our goods. Our goods have been going missing for a long time now." Father said, "Why didn't you tell us this was going on? We would never take any of your goods without asking you first. Those are your goods, not ours. You worked hard for them. Sometimes you share with us and that is good too: but we would never take some without asking first." The children said, "Well, this has been happening for a some time now." Father Mink announced, "I must try to find out who is doing this."

Meanwhile, down at the bay, the tide changed and the water was out. The Cockle clams were proudly sun bathing themselves. They were busy enjoying themselves as they didn't get much of a chance to see Grandfather Sun often. They stuck their noses out to sun until they turned a reddish color. Father Mink walked over to a very large Cockle clam and said, "I have a very troubled mind and I come to you for some answers." The Cockle clam answered, "We know. We know what's been happening. We wondered why you never came to us earlier." Father Mink said, "Because our children thought we'd been borrowing their goods. This is why we didn't come sooner."

The Cockle clam said, "You have very kind children. They look after our children and grandchildren. They only take and appreciate what they really want and need from us. This is why we always give ourselves so willingly to them. The Raccoon children have been coming across here and going into storage holes to steal your children's goods. When they run, their little hands can not hold all the food they take and so it gets scattered on the beach." Father Mink said, "I must go and talk to their father. I am angry at him for letting his children do this." Cockle clam said, "Can you leave this up to us? Please go about doing what you do every morning. When you go out in the morning we will punish them. We won't hurt anyone, but we will punish them. Come back a bit earlier than usual and you will witness their punishment."

Father Mink went to his house and told his wife and children what had happened to their food. The Mink children were relieved and upset at the same time. The youngest Mink said, "Those Raccoons will pay for what they've done, maybe this will teach them not to steal." Father Mink said, "We'll go out early as usual and act normal." They ate their goods first and then went to the pond of salt water along the edge of rocks to wash their hands and faces.

Grandfather Sun was up and it was time to get their baskets. The children followed their parents. Father Mink said to the youngest one, "You be the leader today." The youngest Mink was so happy and started to jump all over. He tripped over his basket and landed on his face. Mother Mink hid her smile and looked away. Father Mink said, "Don't look back my dear children and dear wife, the Raccoon children might be watching and suspect we know what they are up to." So away the Mink family went. They went to the point and started to gather some food. As they walked slowly along the beach, they talked and laughed quietly, even though they were sad to know that someone would steal from them.

S oon after the Mink family left the point, the Raccoon children came into sight. The Cockle clams were watching for them to arrive. This time the Raccoon children didn't walk along the bay, instead they ran across. Mr. Cockle said, "They are very brave now. If they only knew we had a meeting about them this morning." Mr. Cockle had selected the strongest of his children and grandchildren and sent them up to the caves where the Mink family stored their goods in the holes of the rocks. The Cockle family smiled as they watched the Raccoons near the rocks. Mr. Cockle wondered, "Who will be the first to go in the home of the Minks?"

All of a sudden there were screams coming from the cave. "Oooo. Ouch. Let me go. Let me go," screeched the littlest Raccoon. The Raccoons were running and tumbling all over the place. They smashed up against the rocks as they ran screaming from the Mink's food supply. Their parents heard them screaming as they neared the point. They turned around and started running back towards their children's cries. The Raccoon children were slapping and nibbling at what was on their hands. They still rolled around and screamed, "Get this off of me. Let me go. Let me go." The Cockles had clamped themselves onto each of the raccoon's fingers. No matter how hard the Raccoons hit the Cockles they didn't crack or break. They hung on tighter and tighter. Mr.Cockle said, "We will not let you go unless you promise not to steal again." "Get this off me. Get this off me," cried the little Raccoons.

Father Raccoon arrived and demanded that Mr. Cockle let his children go. Mr. Raccoon said, "Why are you doing this to my children? They never do anything to anybody." Mr. Cockle said, "Oh yes they do, they have been stealing from the Mink family." Father Raccoon said, "How could they be stealing when they're sleeping all the time? They do not get up until we get back from getting their food."

Mr. Cockle said, "As soon as you leave they get up and they go across the bay to steal food. They are back in bed by the time you return." Father Raccoon said, "If you let them go I will take them home and punish them myself. They won't even be able to sit down, and their fingers will be broken so they won't be able to steal anymore." Mr. Cockle said, "Is that going to help? Will it stop them from stealing? Or will they get worse? They must promise not to steal anymore and you must promise you will teach them how to get their own goods. You and your wife will have to work very hard to do this."

The Mink family arrived and said, "We will help." Father Raccoon said, "We don't need your help. We will teach them ourselves." "You must let

T he Cockles had clamped themselves onto each of the raccoon's fingers. No matter how hard the Raccoons hit the Cockles they didn't crack or break.

them go. Their fingers will be all crooked by now," cried mother Raccoon. Mr. Cockle nodded towards his children and grandchildren, "Yes, you may release their fingers!" As the Cockles dropped off the Raccoons fingers , the Raccoons continued to cry. The hurt little Raccoons cried, "We will never steal again. We will pay back all the goods we have stolen. We promise to be respectful to others and to the foods as well."

Father Mink said, "We will teach you how to care for your goods." Mother Raccoon said, "I will be very happy if you can help." Mr. Raccoon did not like this at all and said, "You go to the house and stay there Mrs. Raccoon. You will not be helped to do anything." Mr. Cockle said to Mr. Racoon, "The mother of your children is very important and is needed to help raise the children. She is the one who is going to be teaching them how to prepare and respect food and themselves." Mr. Cockle said, "You have littered the beaches with the shells of my cockle children and grandchildren. You didn't appreciate their wealth. I smelled them rotting amongst the rocks by your house."

In the meantime the water rose and said, "When we come back we will help. We will ask the waves to help wash the house." Mother Mink said to mother Raccoon, "I will go with you to get cedar bark. Then we can make beds and mats together." "Oh, Hychqa, Hychqa," replied mother Raccoon. Mother Raccoon was so happy to finally find a friend. Together they left to go to clean the Raccoon house. The water went away too. The Cockles went back into the sand thanking all those who had come to help teach the Raccoon family a lesson. When the tide came in with great big waves, it pushed the garbage laying around the Raccoon house far into the deep sea.

They were all so happy that the Raccoon house was clean. One of the Mink children said, "If you come with us, we will share our goods with

As the Cockles dropped off the Raccoons fingers, the Raccoons continued to cry.

you." Mother Mink said, "We still have a bit of food left. You must bring some here to share with our new friends." The Mink children returned with a few clams and they all ate together. The Mink children showed the Raccoon children how the food must be washed and deposited back into the water where it belongs. They also showed the Raccoons how to remove the shells from the crabs. Everything tasted so good. They all laid together on the rocks and quickly fell asleep with huge smiles on each of their mouths.

Father Mink and father Raccoon came along and looked at the children. They looked so beautiful stretched out on the rocks while Grandfather Sun caressed their bodies. Grandfather Sun also healed the little fingers of the Raccoons as they stuck them up into the air. The two mothers came along with their baskets full of inner cedar bark, which they stripped from the cedar tree. They started to make little mats for their children. Mrs. Mink talked about how important it was to keep their beds clean. When the beds are clean, the ones sleeping on it will be loved and caressed by the cedar mats. This will help the little ones to grow up to be beautiful fathers and mothers.

At the end of the day, the two fathers looked out to sea and smiled with contentment . The two mothers still pulled and stitched the roots of the inner cedar bark into mats. The six little children lay to rest by a cool pool of water. Each member of the Mink and Raccoon family had learned something valuable that day. The Cockles did too, even though they were the ones who had brought the teaching to the Raccoons. They said, "We learned that love can be brought to all people who were involved with problems too big to handle. To this very day you can see that the Raccoon fingers are crooked and stick into the air like they are being healed by Grandfather Sun. This is a reminder to the Raccoons to wash and respect their food.

The Mink children showed the Raccoon children how the food must be washed and deposited back into the water where it belongs.

DEER, RAVEN AND
THE RED SNOW

A long time ago this story was told to teach children not to trick anyone. In this story animals are used as an example to teach children this important lesson.

Early one morning Smuy, the little deer, went to his cupboard and realized there was no more dried salmon, clams, or roots. The only food left was a half basket of his cherished dried blackberries.

Smuy thought to himself, "My food is almost gone. This is all there is! It will be a long time yet before my cousin Salmon swims upstream, and before the Camus and yummy Fern roots grow. MMMmm. I can already taste the white pith of cooked roots and yummy berries. What am I going to do? It is so long yet before summer comes again. My cousin Spaal, the Raven, is always playing tricks on me. Maybe he still has some dried salmon, but he is so stingy. He wouldn't share with me or anyone else. I've given him a lot of food in the past. I know! I'll mash these beautiful berries in the early morning before the sun comes up. I will sing and let my song tell Spaal's brain what I want him to do."

Smuy began to mash the berries and sang his song into the evening, "Feet to the beach, feet to the beach, feet to the beach"

After eating some mixed mashed berries, Smuy went to bed. He was still hungry and tired. His stomach started to growl. He said to his stomach, "Be quiet now. Tomorrow you will be full with dried salmon. I will roast it over the red hot coals so it will be warm and filling." With that thought his

The only food left was a half basket of his cherished dried blackberries.

stomach felt better. With a watery mouth, Smuy drifted off to sleep and dreamt of the beautiful, MMMmm, dried salmon he will have tomorrow.

Smuy was up very early the next morning. He started to drag his basket, which now was almost full of berries and juice, to a spot beneath the cedar trees. He washed his feet, jumped into the basket and started to dance. With every jump Smuy sang "Feet to the beach, feet to the beach, feet to the beach. "Oh! I forgot. I have to go back," Smuy thought to himself as he continued singing, "Feet to the beach, feet to the beach, feet to the beach." "Oh! I think I remember the whole song now." "Take your feet to the beach, take your feet to the beach." Smuy sang the song again and again. As he sang, Smuy remembered Spaal's reaction to noise. Smuy knew that Spaal was curious and when he heard any noise he would fly outside to investigate.

Smuy started to sing below Spaal's tree house, "Take your feet to the beach, feet to the beach, feet to the beach." He stopped singing long enough to grab a big clam shell. Smuy spread the beautiful red berry juice on top of the snow. With the morning wind, everything started to freeze. Smuy tasted the berry juice as he thought, "Yes, yes, it is slowly freezing." He tasted it again and "MMMmm" it was so good.

All of a sudden, the door opened to Spaal's house. "What are you doing out there? What is that song you are singing? Can't you remember anything? You're waking me up with all your noise!" Spaal turned and walked into his house, slammed the door, got into bed and pulled the covers over his head. In his mind, Spaal kept repeating the song, "Feet to the beach, feet to the beach, feet to the beach. Oh I forgot." For a moment, Spaal wondered, "What does that mean?" He barely got any sleep. He awakened with Smuy's song still in his head. "I must get up and look," Spaal said with a yawn.

All of a sudden, the door opened to Spaal's house. "What are you doing out there? What is that song you are singing? Can't you remember anything? You're waking me up with all your noise!"

S paal put some into his mouth, "Ohhh, I like it. I like it. It is so good. MMMmm."

70

Spaal opened his door, and said to Smuy, "My dear cousin, what are you doing? What is that beautiful stuff you are eating? I can't see it. It is too bright for me. Let me have some?" Smuy didn't answer. He kept on working. He cut big chunks of the beautiful red snow and piled it up. Spaal couldn't wait. He came right outside. Even though Spaal's feet would get cold, he was determined to stand outside in the snow until he was able to try some of what Smuy was eating. "I must try what you are eating. Can I have some my dear cousin?" Smuy said, "Oh! alright then. I will let you have a taste and give you some if you like it" Spaal was very excited, "Oh Hychqa, thank you, my cousin. Hychqa." Even before Spaal grabbed for some, his mouth started to drool. Spaal put some into his mouth, "Ohhh, I like it. I like it. It is so good. MMMmm."

Smuy stood and watched Spaal for awhile then said, "This is going to be my food for a long, long time." Spaal said, "Will you please save some for me? And quickly added, "First I have something to do in my house." Smuy said, "Okay, I will keep this side and save this other side for you." Spaal went away nodding, "Hychqa, Hychqa." Spaal went inside his house and started to throw his dried salmon outside. As Spaal threw the dried fish out, he mumbled, "I don't want this smelly, stinky dried salmon. My food from now on will be the beautiful red snow."

Spaal dropped down through the opening at the bottom of his house and started to pack the dried salmon down to the beach. The song 'Feet to the beach' came into Spaal's mind. Spaal liked the song. He packed more fish singing, "Feet to the beach, feet to the beach, feet to the beach." Spaal threw the fish down upon the beach and washed himself off, so Smuy wouldn't smell the fish on him. Spaal finished washing and quickly flew back to his tree house.

Packing his basket and knife, Spaal said to Smuy, "I am here now my dear cousin. I am going to work with you. I will cut and pack my side of the red snow." Smuy said, "Alright. I too have some work to do. I will be gone for awhile. But I will be back to finish my job." Smuy went back to his house and climbed through the back window. He raced down towards the beach. He said with a big grin, "I knew it! I knew it! Look at all the beautiful dried salmon Spaal has thrown away. It's going to be all mine!" Smuy packed the dried salmon and carried it up to the back window of his house.

Comfortably inside his house, Smuy piled the dried salmon and built a fire. He started to roast the dried salmon. Smuy stood in front of the fire and said, "Oh, it smells so good! I can't wait to eat fish again. Stomach, you will be full with dried salmon soon enough. Ah! it's time to try some of this fresh roasted dried salmon. MMMmm, it tastes so good." After licking the last bit of crumbs from his hooves, Smuy laid down and fell asleep.

In the meantime, Spaal was busy working and eating at the same time. He would eat, then cut a few chunks of the red snow and put it into his basket then eat some more. After Spaal finished cutting half of his side of the red snow, he dragged his basket up into his tree house. Spaal came back down to finish gathering his side of the red snow. He thought he might as well sneak a bit more from Smuy's side too. He started to cut into Smuy's pile. Spaal was so tricky. He gathered more white snow and spread what little was left of the red snow from Smuy's pile on top of it. This made Smuy's pile look bigger than it really was. After Spaal finished sneaking around and cutting his side of the red snow, he drug his basket up into his tree house.

S paal was so tricky. He gathered more white snow and spread what little was left of the red snow on top of it.

This made Smuy's pile look bigger than it really was.

Spaal had filled all four corners of his tree house with the red snow. The only open space left was in the middle of the floor. Spaal drug his bed to the open space and sat and thought, "I will be fine here. I'm not going anywhere. I'll stay here and eat my red snow. Who needs anyone or anything else? Now that I have this beautiful food I'm happy just the way I am." He ate a litte more red snow then slowly drifted off to sleep. Spaal was so happy and content with his delicious red snow, he could barely sleep. Just thinking about the red snow made his mouth water. He propped up and cut off a little more of the red snow. "MMMmm, this is so tasty," he said with a smile.

Smuy knocked on Spaal's door. As the door opened, Smuy said, "I'm sorry cousin. I went to sleep. I was very tired from singing. I thought if I sang, the red snow would be happy. I wanted the red snow to be happy when you ate it." Spaal said, "Hychqa. Hychqa. I am so thankful to you. I am also very full and tired too. I will return the favour to you one day. But for now I to am off to rest for awhile." Smuy hid his face as he went away laughing. "I fooled him. I fooled him. He ate the red snow, and he liked it so much that he didn't like his dried salmon anymore. I sure did fool him. Ha Ha Ha Ha."

Spaal smiled and said to himself, "I am so warm and happy, I"m going to go to sleep." He snuggled into his little pillow and dozed off to sleep. Not to long into his sleep Spaal awakened shivering cold. Clutching his little bark pillow he mumbled, "What is wrong? It is so cold in here. What did I do with the kindling? Oh yes! I had it under my bed in the corner." He crawled to the corner and dragged some kindling out across the floor. Still mumbling to himself Spaal said, "I'll only need a little bit of wood for the fire." He laid beside the fire and went back to sleep. He woke again. This time he reached up and put a little piece of red snow in his mouth. "MMMmm" Spaal said, as he rubbed his eyes and drifted back to sleep.

Spaal awakened in the middle of the night. It was cold and dark. He crawled to the corner to get more kindling. Then he started to rebuild the fire. It was hard for Spaal to roll the sticks between his hands. His hands were cold and frozen but he continued to roll the sticks. Finally, the fire started. He built the fire bigger this time. His hands and feet started to feel warm. He kept turning around and around to warm his backside and feet. After a few turns around the fire, Spaal reached up and grabbed for more red snow. Spaal was happy and felt warm as he snuggled up to sleep.

Towards morning Smuy heard somebody screaming. He ran outside. The screaming came from his cousin's house. "I'd better go see what is wrong," thought Smuy. It was Spaal hollering, "Open the door. Open the door." Smuy forced the door open. Out came Spaal floating on a torrent of red water. His little legs and arms were sticking up in the air. Spaal was screaming, "Save me. Save me. I am drowning. I don't know where this water came from. It's all red. Where did the red water come from?"

Smuy said, "I don't know my dear cousin. I heard you and came running to save you." Spaal said, "Hychqa. Hychqa, for saving me. I would have drowned if you hadn't come. That awful red water. Where did it come from? Somebody must have put it in there. Did it rain last night?" Smuy said, "I don't know. I don't think so. I just wanted to come help you. When I heard you screaming I thought you needed help."

muy forced the door open. Out came Spaal floating on a torrent of red water. His little legs and arms were sticking up in the air.

While Spaal sat there drying and shaking himself off, he said, "Hychqa. You are always so kind." Smuy said, "Come to my house my dear cousin. I will make you a nice warm drink. I still have some dried salmon too. I will roast some for us on the fire." Spaal said, "Don't mention fire! My fire is out due to all that red water." Smuy said, "That's okay. You can build the fire again." He guided his cousin towards his house.

When they got there, Smuy set Spaal on a nice mat close to the warm fire. Smuy took some hot rocks from the fire with two spare sticks and lowered them into a basket of water. Shortly after the hot rocks had been placed into the basket, the water started to boil. Smuy tested the water and felt that it was ready to make their drinks. Smuy said, "I will put some elderberry in the hot water for tea. We will have a hot calming drink. You have been through a lot my dear cousin."

Smuy went to the corner and opened a box which was half filled with dried fish. Spaal said, "I thought you didn't have anymore fish." Smuy replied, "I didn't. I traded our cousin Seal for some of her dried salmon." Smuy continued to roast the dried salmon. Spaal said, "I am the only one that makes this kind of fish. I am the only one that can dry salmon like that. I would know my dried salmon anywhere."

Smuy continued to smile and smacked his lips. Thinking to himself, "Spaal hasn't even asked what happened to his house, nor has he thought to go and look at it." He gave Spaal some of the dried salmon. When Spaal ate it he said, "Oh, I am so hungry. MMMmm, this is so good. I thought I was the only one that could make dried salmon like this. My dear cousin I have no more dried salmon in my house. Would you, could you...would you be so kind enough to share a bit of your dried salmon with me?"

Smuy said, "Oh, I think I can do that. I will give you some when I take you home." Spaal said, "Oh, Hychqa, Hychqa, my dear cousin."

When Smuy took Spaal home, Spaal didn't say anything about his house except, "Oh it is so clean in here. It smells so good. It smells like berries. Hychqa for the bundle of dried salmon. Hychqa, my cousin. Hychqa." Smuy left Spaal's side and returned home.

S muy continued to roast the dried salmon.